MY VERY FIRST SIMBA STORIES

Disney's

NOT SO FAST!

Written by Ellen Weiss   Illustrated by Robbin Cuddy

Printed in the United States of America.

FIRST EDITION
1 3 5 7 9 10 8 6 4 2

Library of Congress Catalog Card Number: 99-067854
ISBN: 0-7868-3266-5

For more Disney Press fun, visit www.disneybooks.com

MY VERY FIRST SIMBA STORIES

Disney's

NOT SO FAST!

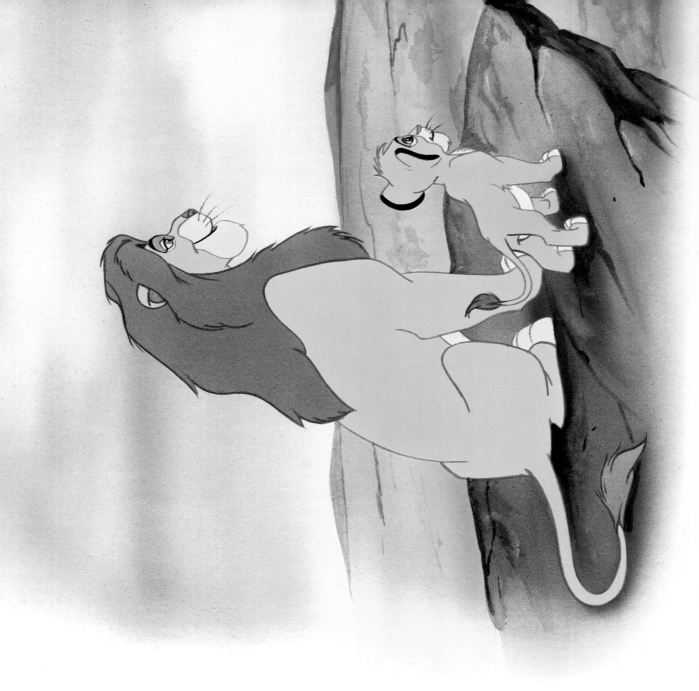

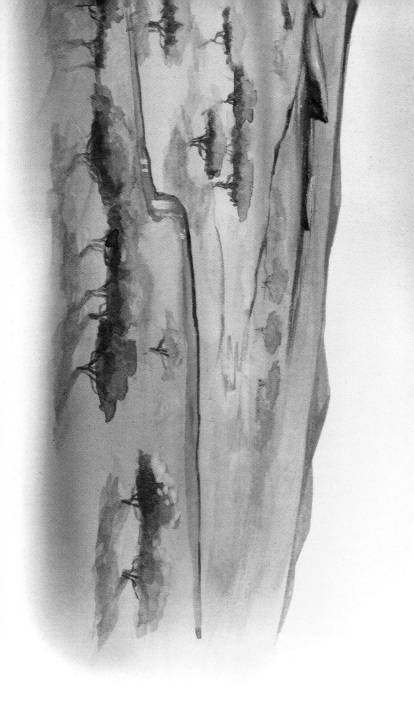

Simba was going to be king one day. He knew that.

But right now his father, Mufasa, was king of the Pride Lands.

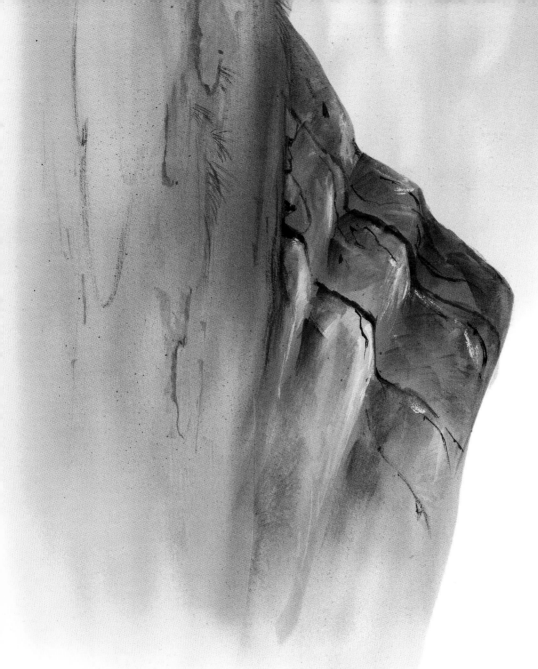

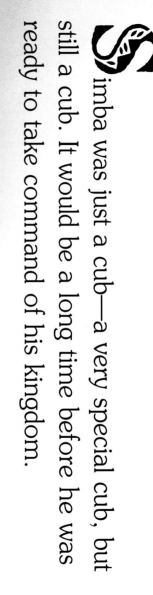

Simba was just a cub—a very special cub, but still a cub. It would be a long time before he was ready to take command of his kingdom.

His elders were always trying to teach him things, so he would be a good king.

Mufasa took him for a walk. "Look, son," he said. "Everything that the sun touches will be yours someday."

"Yes, Dad," Simba said. But he was watching a line of ants marching toward their anthill.

"Simba, pay attention!" Mufasa said.

Zazu took him out to Antelope Hill to see the sunrise.

But Simba did not keep up. He was watching a nightjar singing in a tree.

"Why do you dawdle so?" Zazu said in exasperation. "We'll miss the sunrise!"

"But look at that bird!" Simba said.

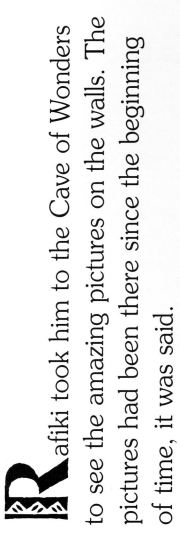

Rafiki took him to the Cave of Wonders to see the amazing pictures on the walls. The pictures had been there since the beginning of time, it was said.

But it was well past lunchtime when they got there. The whole way there, Simba was busy trying to pounce on a grasshopper.

Rafiki just smiled and shook his head.

"Simba," said his mother, "why do you dawdle all the time? You're always looking at some little thing, and we never get anywhere!"

"But I like the little things, and we never get anywhere!"

"But I like the little things, Mom," said Simba.

"Let's not go so fast."

His mother smiled.

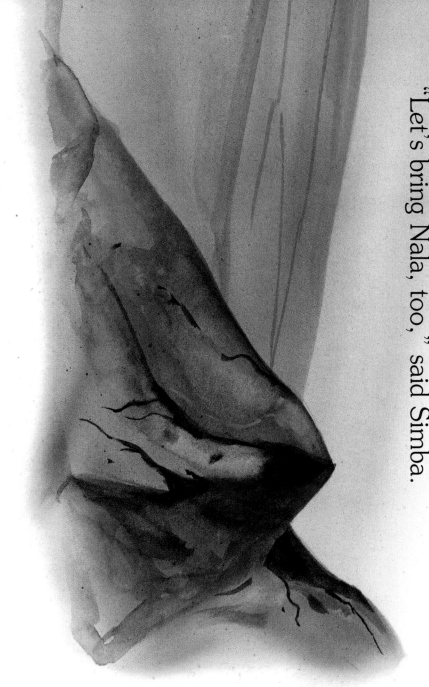

ne day, Zazu woke Simba up early.

"Time to get up, Master Simba," said Zazu.

"We'll be going on a long, long walk today."

"Why?" Simba asked, sleepily rubbing his eyes.

"Your father has asked me to show you the farthest part of the Pride Lands," said Zazu.

"Let's bring Nala, too," said Simba.

"**L**ook at your kingdom," said Zazu. "Isn't it grand?"

"Mm-hmm," said Simba. "Hey, Nala, look at this neat purple pebble."

"Please, Master Simba," Zazu pleaded. "We have a long way to go. You can't dawdle so much!"

"Awww, Zazu," said Simba, "this mud is so much fun!"

"**G**o 'way, bee," said Nala, waving her paw. "I hate bees!"

"We must respect all creatures, from the buzzing bee to the leaping antelope," said Zazu.

"Even the hyenas?" asked Simba.

"I hate hyenas!" said Nala with a shudder. "They're scary!"

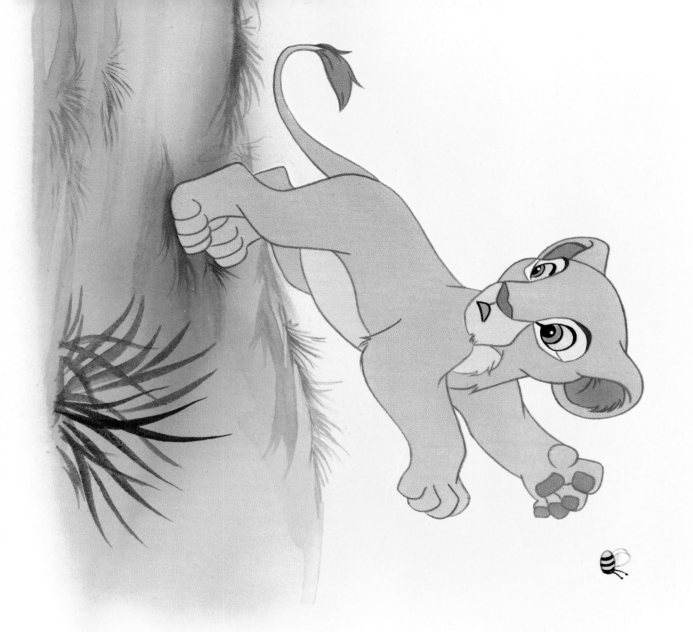

They kept on going, on and on. Zazu kept talking about all the things Simba would rule one day.

"Mmm-hmmm!" said Simba. "Hey, look at this stick. It's shaped like a lizard! And look at these, Zazu!"

"Certainly not," harrumphed Zazu. "We have important business today! No time to look at every little thing!"

"**N**o!" said Simba. "Look at this—I order you!" He made his voice as princely as possible.

"Yes, Master Simba," sighed Zazu. He bent over to see what Simba was looking at.

"Hyena tracks!" yelped Zazu. "Good heavens! We've strayed out of the Pride Lands! We must hurry home!"

But it was too late. The hyenas had spotted them.

"Run, Master Simba! Run, Nala!" Zazu cried.

"Run toward home!"

They all took off, going as fast as they could. Behind them, the hyenas followed.

"**B**ack to the Pride Lands! Head for the far side of the watering hole!" squawked Zazu. "If they follow us there, they'll have to answer to your father!"

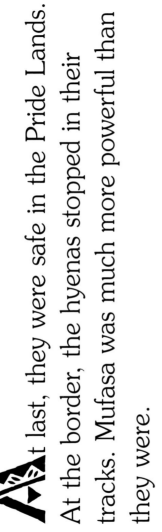

At last, they were safe in the Pride Lands.

At the border, the hyenas stopped in their tracks. Mufasa was much more powerful than they were.

"Thank goodness you saw those footprints, Master Simba," said Zazu.

Shaking, they walked the rest of the way home. "I don't know what came over me," Zazu apologized. "I was so busy looking at the big things, I forgot to look at the little ones!"

guess it was pretty lucky you had me along, right, Zazu?" said Simba.

"It certainly was, Master Simba," said Zazu.

"It was lucky indeed."

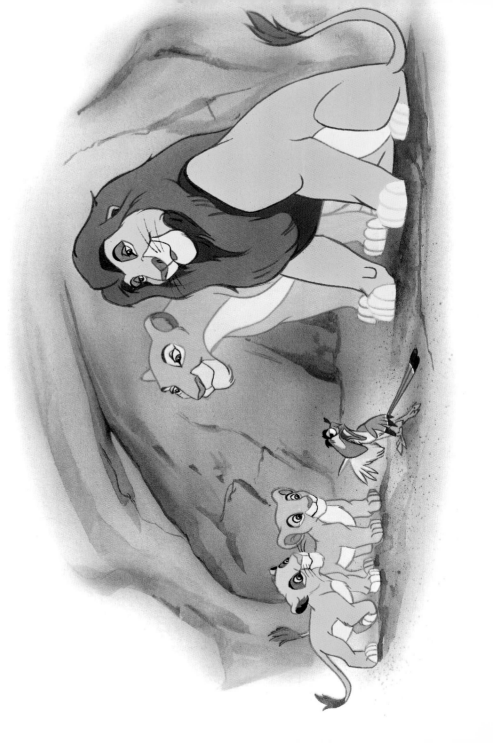